CRAZY

Natoya Palmer

Case Number (Copyright Registration ID): 1-15015707011

ISBN:
Paperback: 978-1-971141-07-7
Hardcover: 978-1-971141-08-4

Published by: Columbus Book Publishers

www.columbusbookpublishers.com/

Printed in the United States of America

Dedication

I want to thank my mother, my deceased father, my two beautiful daughters, my sisters, my nieces, and my nephews. I love you.

Table of Contents

Page Left Blank Intentionally

Chapter One

"What have we done, Kim? We just up and left our babies? I didn't even kiss him goodbye either!"

"Bitch, stop crying about them goddamn kids! Jackie's long-head ass will be there to kiss his little ass whenever he starts to cry. That bitch Jackie should have raised her cum-sucking son better, and she wouldn't have gotten left with her grandsons. Do you know how many times a day Bill done threatened me and said that as soon as the babies were born, he was kicking all of us out? I had to show that motherfucka that he done fucked with the wrong bitch. I can go, but my son will always be a part of that money, and if walking away from my son makes me a terrible person, then I guess I'm a terrible person. Men are always walking the fuck away from their kids. I just left first, and I don't give a fuck! Ashley, do you think that son of a bitch cared that he was fucking me, and you, and passed Megan to an old, decrepit father just because he's rich and powerful? Bill and his entire family can suck my fucking dead dog's dick. Like I said, Bill better take care of our son, and have a coke and a smile, and shut the fuck up!"

"Kim, do you think something is wrong with the bus? My bus was supposed to pull up thirty minutes ago! Kim, your bus is even running late! I wonder what's holding up our bus, Kim? Toya and Tara are gonna start fucking with me soon. I can just hear them now. 'Mommy, I'm hungry. I got to go to the bathroom.' I can't stand all that whining and shit. My little fools are always acting out. Motherfuckers act like they ain't got no home training.

Motherfuckers better get their shit together. Mom ain't too pleased about us coming back home. Stud arrived home two weeks ago. Stud been calling, talking about Momma been talking bad about us. Calling us black trash. Stud is ready to cuss her ass smoove out."

"Ashley, fuck your dick-head ass son."

"Kim, watch your mouth talking about my boy. Stud could be your son's possible daddy."

"Ashley, your boy ran like a little bitch. Stud ain't even leave his possible bastard one red penny. He can go to hell!"

"Stud only left because Bill kept threatening him. My son wanted to help you with the baby."

"Your son is a bastard, and he wasn't gonna help me do shit. Fuck you, Kim. You're the one that told Stud the baby wasn't his."

"Ashley, I told all them fools that they were the pappy! I really don't give a fuck about no nothing-ass man. To tell you the truth, Ashley, all of them could be my baby's father. I was fucking them all raw dog. Let me remind you about life, Ashley, as long as I'm still Mrs. King, my son will remain a King. I left my little problem with the right motherfuckers. Damn, Kim, I'm wondering what the hold-up with this late-ass bus is? I knew I should have caught the train. Damn, I spent all my money on these bus tickets, and them motherfuckers take their slow-ass time. I'm about to go to customer service so I can complain. I know Tony is waiting patiently for me to arrive."

Before she could go to customer service and cuss their ass out, Jackie's bat-shit crazy ass came out of nowhere. This bitch Jackie grabbed me by the back of my hair and shoved me to the ground. Ashley's old, dumb ass froze up like a little punk bitch. She didn't even try to help me whoop her ass either.

"Look at the fleas on you dirty bitches! Y'all really got me fucked up! Kim, was your dirty ass on your way to customer service worrying about why the bus has been delayed? I delayed the motherfucking bus, bitch. This is my town, and nothing moves without my say-so. I should have known your old crazy self had something to do with the bus delay."

"Shut up, bitch. I came all this way to destroy your plans, Kim. Tony won't be waiting for you. Ashley, your mother won't be welcoming your nasty ass back home. To be honest with you hoes, I paid them off. I also made sure that y'all would be blacklisted in every state, and since I'm known worldwide, your tricking ass won't even be welcomed in Paris, Kim. Now get y'all's bum ass up out of my town and don't ever come back. Y'all some dirty, fucked-up-in-the-head-ass cunts."

Chapter Two

I should have known Jackie's crazy ass was gonna try and run up on us. That bitch Jackie just had to rub it in our faces that we're broke.

"I'm scared, Kim. My intention was to go back to New York City and live off Momma for a couple of months. Jackie's nasty ass done messed up everything. Kim, I only have ten dollars in my pocket to spare. Toya and Tara will be up in a minute, hungry and thirsty, begging for every damn thing."

"Ashley, you mean to tell me that you only have ten dollars to rub together? Ashley, I don't mean no harm or disrespect, but you have been fucking and sucking my husband's dick all this time, and you only have ten dollars? Ashley, you sure is a good-for-nothing type of bitch. Bitch, you're gonna have to wise the fuck up, because where we are about to go, you're gonna need a brain, some fire pussy, and your dick-sucking skills need to be over the top."

"What the fuck is you talking about, Kim? I have no place for myself or my girls, and you're talking about some other shit."

"That's why you and the girls are coming with me to Texas."

"Texas? What's in Texas, Kim?"

"Rich men with money, and lots of it. I plan on buying an old dump and fixing it up, and turning it into a hoe house. Shit, all this free pussy I gave to my husband, somebody's gonna pay for my time being wasted. We gonna make so much money, Ashley. All we need is at least four tricks to fund us until we start making money. Once we start making money, we can start tricking, and then we can find us some hoes to start tricking, and then we can sit on our ass and let them suck and fuck all day."

"Kim, you really have a wild imagination. Kim, aren't you upset with Tony for fronting on you?"

"Hell no, fuck him. One motherfucker don't stop no show. That motherfucker is married anyway. Let's go to customer service and get these tickets changed to Texas. I wonder what Megan is doing? That bitch got it made in the shade. I give her props for getting pregnant by Eric. Megan will never be broke again, thanks to her little bastard that she brought into the world. I bet Jackie's crazy ass will be sending Megan away soon as she can think of a small island to ditch her off to. Jackie ain't dumb. She knows Eric loves that pussy. If I was Jackie, I would be sending my husband's hoe away too."

"I hope we're not making a big mistake by going all the way to Texas, Kim."

"We're not, Bitch! Just understand the fucking assignment. Fuck, suck, and get the money. Ashley, don't go to Texas and go falling in love with one of them fuck boys either. Just stay focused on the task."

Out of nowhere, a handsome police officer walked up to us and asked where we were headed. "Texas, sir. Are we in any kind of trouble or something?"

"No, I was just being nosy."

"Well, Officer, since you're so concerned for our whereabouts, come invest in some of this good pussy before we get on the bus."

"How much you charging, baby?"

"A hundred dollars for a thirty-minute fuck, and fifty dollars for your dick to be sucked."

"I don't have time for no fucking, but I will take advantage of my dick getting wet."

"Sounds like a plan, Officer. Ashley, get your ass up and go suck some dick. Your girls will be hungry in a while, and you only stole ten dollars from my husband's cheap ass."

Chapter Three

"Momma, did you find them stanking-ass hoes? These spoiled babies keep crying and spitting up. I'm not cut out to be nobody's full-time daddy. I definitely need a blood test for both babies. Those little bastards don't look like me either."

"Bill, you sound worse than a little kid. Bill, those boys are yours, and you're gonna take care of them. Bill, this is what you get for marrying a slut and whoring around with the maid. Son, this is your karma. And another thing, please stop calling my grandkids monsters. Their names are Bill Junior and Corey, and don't you forget it. I did run into your kids' mothers. Those hoes won't be coming back for their babies anytime soon. You're gonna have to become a momma and daddy, so get used to it. Bill, you have no choice but to grow up and finally become the man that I raised you to be, instead of acting like a man whore."

"So, Momma, what in the hell are you gonna do about Daddy's new daughter? Momma, you still got me and Daddy's whore living right here in the family home."

"Bill, this whole mess started because you and that slut of a wife you got had to have extra people in your bedroom, and your father got beside himself and got tricked by lust. Anyways, Eric will always take care of his responsibilities. I have fallen completely in love with Megan's baby, and for some strange reason, I have grown very fond of Megan. Megan has had a terrible childhood, and she's still young, she just turned eighteen, you know. Bill, I still can't believe how you and your father took full advantage of Megan."

"Listen, Momma, I'm never gonna cry over spilled milk or an overpriced whore. Anyway, Momma, I'm gonna have at least two nannies for these little monsters. I can't watch them twenty-four/seven. I have to work, remember?"

"I'm not paying for a goddamn thing. Bill, your sorry ass is employed on the property, where your children are located. With that being said, when your sorry ass reports to work, your babies will be accompanying you."

"Momma, I can't take them with me to work. What will the employees think?"

"They'll think that you're a single father that doesn't have anyone to watch his children. I promise you, son, you will have a better bond with your boys if you keep them close by you."

"I still can't believe this shit, Momma? I'm about to take care of someone else's kids that aren't even mine. Please hurry up and arrange for the paternity test so I can prove to you that them little monsters aren't mine. I have to do it soon, because you know what they say: You start feeding them bastards, and they'll start looking like you."

"Eric, we have to hurry up before Jackie catches us laying here butterball naked."

"Jackie knows better than to come up to my private room, questioning me. My wife knows that you're my woman and the mother of my beautiful daughter, and nobody comes between that."

"Eric, I'm starting to feel really awful about fucking on you while Mrs. King is downstairs. Jackie's been so kind to me. She almost treated me like a friend."

"I think that's wonderful, Megan. I'm really happy you and my wife are getting along because I need and love both of you. Megan, you don't need to worry about Jackie; she knows that I'll never leave her for anybody. Megan, my dear, let's stop talking about my wife. I really need for you to start sucking my dick. I'm really horny."

"Eric, the doctor said it will take another week for my pussy to heal up."

"I can't wait no week. I need you right now, Megan."

She was about to give Eric's old, whining ass some of her good loving, but she could have sworn that she saw Jackie's shadow. "Damn, how am I gonna suck Eric's dick now, knowing Jackie's nosy ass is watching?"

Chapter Four

Just when I thought I had a few minutes in the movie room by myself, here comes Bill's hating ass following behind me.

"What's going on, whore? I guess you think you got it made in the shade. You've done pussy-whipped my father, and you got my mother thinking you're some type of innocent whore who needs to be saved."

"I'm sorry, Bill, for coming to your family's home and causing so much pain. Bill, I thought you were gonna send me back home in three months, but instead, Eric knocked me up. I never thought that I would be carrying your father's sucker. I truly do hate that I have hurt your mother, this was never my intention."

"Shut the fuck up, whore. With all them damn lies. You're an evil bitch, just like them skanks that left me with their bastards. Oh, and don't ever think that my father or mother really gives three fucks about your ragged whore ass either."

Before I got a chance to turn around and leave the movie room, Bill grabbed me by the neck with one hand and placed his whole hand in my vagina. I was so scared. I really thought that he wanted to kill me, so I kept letting him pleasure me until he calmed down and released his hand from my throat. Men are so crazy. While pleasuring me, all he kept asking repeatedly was if his dick was better than Eric's. To be honest, Bill's penis was much better than Eric's. Before I knew it, I came all over Bill's hand.

"Just like I thought, you ain't nothing but a dirty slut. Don't you forget who the fuck I am, Megan? Don't ever forget you're my whore. Now get your filthy ass up out of my movie room before my father and mother come home and find you sucking my dick in their home."

As I started to run out of the movie room, I heard Bill laughing and taunting me, calling me a "fucking whore."

While on my way upstairs, I walked past my baby's room and had no real desire to even go in there to check on her, or even tell her that I loved her, which was a little bit fucked up. While I was trying to creep into my room, Jackie crept up behind me and scared the shit out of me.

"Is there a problem, Megan? I saw you walk past baby Maya's room, and it looked like you had no good intention to stop and check on her."

"Jackie, Maya was sleeping so good, I didn't wanna disturb her. Jackie, I really don't mean to be a bother, but did you get in contact with any of them schools that you promised me I could attend?"

"I haven't gotten around to checking on any schools, Megan. I've been so busy with all of these babies and new staff around here, I feel like I'm getting overwhelmed."

"I really didn't mean to be a bother, Jackie."

"Megan, you're never a bother. I actually enjoy your company. Megan, I was really hoping you might want to stick around for a while. You just gave birth to Maya, and to be honest, me and Eric will miss you. We're so used to seeing your face around the house. You have brought a huge amount of joy and love to my home."

"You're so kind to me, Jackie, even though I really don't deserve it."

"I was gonna give you this necklace later on, but I think right now's a good time."

Ms. Jackie pulled out a pair of ten-carat gold earrings out of this red heart-shaped box. "Oh, my goodness, Jackie, I love them."

"Megan, I'm overjoyed that you're loving your new earrings. Megan, let me see how they look on you."

While I was putting the earrings on, I could tell Jackie was kind of looking at me a little funny, and it made me nervous.

"Wow, you look beautiful, Megan. I'm gonna go buy you some new clothes tomorrow to go with your earrings. How does that sound, beautiful?"

Before I could thank her, Jackie starts to kiss me passionately on the lips. I was so in shock and a little bit scared. Jackie must have seen my shocked face, and then she planted one last kiss on my hand, and before she left the room, she told me that she was falling in love with me. All I could think about in my fucked-up mind was how bat-shit crazy these people really were. I really needed to get the fuck out of this house before the whole family considered running a damn train on me.

Chapter Five

After turning down at least ten "for sale" properties, we finally found a livable fixer-upper.

"Kim, I can't stay here. This house has roaches, and I can tell this house has a few rats running around here."

"Ashley, all we need to do is buy some boric acid, and I'm sure we can find a stray cat lurking outside for the rats. Bitch, we'll be fine. Just think, with some extra cleaning and some of that mouth-watering food you be cooking, this house will feel like home real soon. Ashley, I'm not gonna fund a fool, you're gonna work this off, bitch. You can start by cleaning first. Anyway, I need to go into town so I can pick up some groceries, and hopefully I might find me a trick."

"What's a trick, Aunty Kim?"

"Well, a trick is a foolish-ass man that doesn't know what to do with his money, so Aunty Kim gracefully takes pleasure in helping him spend it. Toya, we'll talk about these tricking-ass men later. For now, I need you and your sister to grab the bleach and a towel and get to cleaning, is that understood?"

"Yes, Aunty Kim."

On my way back from the grocery store, I ran into this cute-looking man that almost sent me flying on the ground.

"Hey, motherfucker, watch where the fuck you're going, you piece of shit."

"Oh my goodness, beautiful, I have this surgery that I'm trying to get to, and I'm in a rush."

"I'm not fucked up about your surgeries, just watch where the fuck you're going next time."

"You must be new here? What's your name, sweet thing?"

"Money. I don't have time for small talk."

"My name is Jordan, and I would love to take you out, if you're not busy."

"Listen, Jordan, I'm not trying to be rude or anything, but my time is money. I charge for my time."

After explaining my sex rates to Jordan, he seemed like he was super interested, so I told him that I would be cool if he could come through. I also told him I had another hoe at the house that could use a date also. Jordan's fine ass was so excited to tell me that his brother-in-law would be the perfect match for Ashley.

Just when I thought I was on my way home, I ran up on this local club that was loudly playing The Isley Brothers. All I could think about was how thirsty I had gotten from talking to my new little trick, Jordan. My sexy self was feeling so good, I decided to treat myself to a double shot of Hennessy.

As I downed my last shot of Hennessy, this little short, light-skinned man walked up to me.

"Hey, sexy, I never saw you before? You just moved here?"

"That's none of your fucking business."

"My name is Kenny, what's your name, honey?"

"My name is Money, and if you don't have a bunch of it, keep it pushing, shorty doe-whop."

"Money, you came to the right spot. How much you charging?"

After running game on Kenny's short ass, I had enough to buy me and Ashley some sexy clothes to wear around the house. I also informed Kenny that I worked twenty-four/seven and if he had any friends that were interested in a threesome to stop over.

Damn, I was really overjoyed to have made it home. Just like I thought, Ashley don't cooked up a feast, and the house smelled like bleach and Pine-Sol.

"Aunty Kim, we found a kitten lurking in the backyard. I don't think he belongs to anyone. Can we keep it?"

"Well, I guess, because I think we have a few mice. Momma done set up a few traps and killed at least three baby mice. Momma also poured boric acid almost everywhere."

"If the mouse traps or kitten don't get rid of all this credence, then that boric acid will definitely do the job. Come to the table, everybody, dinner's done."

While enjoying our feast, Toya's annoying ass brought up when the babies were coming to live with us. I wanted Toya and Tara to understand that them mistakes weren't welcomed in this house and that they were with their no-good-ass daddy.

Chapter Six

"Ashley, come downstairs. Our money makers are here."

"What are their names, Kim?"

"Don't know. What I do know is that he's a doctor and his brother-in-law is some type of investment banker."

We got comfortable with each other, and I could tell that the trick wanted to make small talk. So I had to let their cheating ass know that they weren't on some sort of date.

"Listen up, time is money, and I have another trick after you, so let's get this party started. I'm ready to make some money."

I was so shocked at how big his penis was. His dick had to be at least twelve inches. When I tried to deep-throat him, I literally got choked. Then this motherfucker did the unthinkable. He was choking my neck and started ramming his big dick back and forth in my mouth like he lost his mind. After that, he must get off on his dick being sucked, and he came in my mouth like he enjoyed every minute of my good loving.

"Did you enjoy yourself, Kim?"

"No, I didn't. Your dick is the size of a grown man's shoe. Motherfucker, I'm gonna have to charge you extra for that mandingo dick you're slanging around."

"Why are you looking at me like I'm gonna bite you? This is my first time whoring for money, and I'm a little nervous."

"Wow, this is some funny-ass shit. Girl, I've been with a dozen whores, and you're the first one that told me that she was nervous. Today is your lucky day, Ashley. I bought some coke before I came here, and maybe if you try some, you won't feel so nervous."

"I've never done drugs in my whole life, and I don't intend to."

"Well, you're gonna have to liven the fuck up, because you're boring. I like for my freaks to appear like they're enjoying themselves."

"Maybe I'll try a little bit to knock the edge off."

Once the coke entered my system, I was hooked, and for once, I felt at peace with myself. I was no longer nervous. I was ready for the assignment. I fucked the shit out of whatever his name is and wore his boney ass out. My little trick was so pleased, he gave me an extra fifty dollars for my services.

"I'm gonna have to see you again, Ashley?"

"I would love your company again. Make sure you bring some more cocaine, handsome?"

"Ashley, baby, the way you ate my ass out, I'll bring you as much coke as you like."

Damn, it felt wonderful having money, knowing I can buy the twins some clothes. My plan was to send my baby boy some money. I instantly started feeling ashamed, and I started missing my baby that I left at Jackie's house. Lucky for me, my trick left me a small dose of coke on the dresser. Fuck it, I was back to feeling no pain once I sniffed my new drug of choice.

While enjoying my high, I got interrupted by this strange noise outside. Our neighbors were hiding packages that appeared to be coke. Since I was super nosy tonight, I could have sworn I saw a large quantity of cocaine. Let me find out, our new neighbors were drug dealers. I hope our new neighbors don't mind sharing some of their dope.

Chapter Seven

"Damn, it seems like I just fed and changed this baby. Maya sure is getting on my last nerve. She's always fucking needy, and I really think Jackie done spoiled Maya so bad. Whenever I put her down, she cries for no reason."

While rocking Maya for the fiftieth time, I looked outside and could've sworn I saw my mother watching from outside. Just when I was about to go outside to see if that was, in fact, my mother, Bill came out of nowhere.

"Hey, whore, are you ready for some real dick?"

"Bill, I was on my way outside. I can't talk right now."

Just as I was about to walk away, Bill grabbed me by my hair and swung me to the ground.

"Bitch, I'm tired of you acting like you're some sort of prize. Bitch, you think you're important, don't you? You're a fucking whore, and I'm gonna treat you as such. Get on your knees, hoe!"

"Bill, Eric and Jackie will be coming home soon. I know you don't want them to walk in and find you raping me."

"Bitch, fuck you! Get on your fucking knees, you dirty whore."

Before I could get on my knees, Bill already had his big penis hanging outside of his pants. I closed my eyes and started sucking Bill's dick like it was a sucker or popsicle. My over-the-top dick-sucking skills were good to him because he came in my mouth in less than a minute.

"Now bend over, I'mma show you again what real dick feels like."

After repeatedly trying several times to stop Bill from violating me, I just gave up and let him have his way. Shit, after a few hard strokes, I started enjoying every minute of Bill's hardcore sex. Just as soon as I was about to cum, Bill's stanking ass pulled out of my vagina.

"Get up, Bitch. Momma and my father will be home soon. Make sure you wash your ass and brush your teeth, you nasty cunt. Next time, whore, I'll have you get some fruit and let you eat it off my dick. I bet you'd like that."

"Okay, Bill, we can do whatever you like."

"Megan, hurry up and kick rocks before I put my dick down your throat once again."

While gathering my clothes, Bill grabbed me by the neck and told me that my pussy will always be his. While running my bathwater, Momma came from out of nowhere and scared the shit out of me.

"Momma, what are you doing here? If Eric and Jackie catch you on their property, they'll put you in jail."

"Fuck them, they ain't gonna do shit. I missed you, Megan, and I wanted to inform you that your father passed away a week ago."

"I'm sorry to hear about Daddy."

"Megan, fuck him too, that tired motherfucker needed to die. Megan, you better not shed a tear for that piece of shit. Let that sorry motherfucker go straight to hell."

"What will you do with yourself now Daddy's passed away?"

"Find me a pimp with some fire dope, what the fuck you think I'm do? I'll be okay, don't worry about me. So what's going on between you and Jackie's son? I thought you were fucking the father? I saw you downstairs with his dick in your mouth and you almost seemed like you were enjoying yourself. I was surprised you didn't wake up the baby, you was moaning so loud."

"Damn, Momma, you was being way too nosy. Momma, it's not none of your business or anything. I'm still Eric's woman."

"So Bill took the pussy, Megan?"

"Momma, Bill's been threatening me for a while now. I just gave in to his twisted desire. I just couldn't keep him off me. I feel awful, Momma. I decided just to give him some of this good pussy and maybe he would leave me the fuck alone."

"Megan, you definitely don't know men. You deep-throated that sucker so good, I thought he was gonna have a seizure. I bet you Bill tries to get pussy by tomorrow. Momma, what am I supposed to do? Eric will be pissed if he finds out that I let Bill fuck on me?"

"Megan, fuck him being mad, tell his old ass to pay you double of whatever he's paying you to keep your legs closed. Make sure you charge Bill's stank ass next time."

"I hope it doesn't become a next time."

"Anyway, while Bill was dicking you down, I stole two thousand dollars from him. I'm gonna give it to you, but the next time I catch you fucking on anybody and not getting paid, I'm beat your ass. Megan, do I make myself clear?"

"Yes, Momma."

"I was thinking now that your daddy is dead, maybe me and you can go in business with each other."

"Business doing what, Momma?"

"I was thinking maybe we can go down south and set up shop there. We'll be making crazy money in no time."

"Momma, I'm not going down south, I have a baby by Eric and Jackie's sending me to college soon."

"Megan, get your dumb ass out the clouds. Jackie ain't sending you nowhere. Jackie's ass thinks she's slick, she only wants to eat your box and watch you and her husband from time to time have sex.

"Mom, how do you know all of our business?"

"I've been watching this house for a long time now. Y'all motherfuckers have been doing a lot of nasty shit in this house. No wonder it's three babies in the house and they're born the same day."

"Momma, you have to go, I think I hear Jackie and Eric pulling up."

"I'll be back to check on you and my grandbaby. I don't trust these people, they're batty for real."

"Okay, Momma, hurry up and get the fuck out before Eric and Jackie catch you here."

Chapter Eight

While trying to rest my body, Eric and Jackie came walking into my bedroom. I instantly got nervous because I thought they were coming to cuss me out.

"Megan, we've got some wonderful news. My brother and his family will be coming to visit tomorrow. We wanted you to look like a million bucks, so we picked you up some new dresses."

Before I could get out a thank you, Jackie abruptly came up to me and kissed me on the lips, right in front of Eric. I could tell Eric was caught off guard.

"Eric, I didn't mean to shock you, but I'm starting to catch feelings for Megan."

"Have you lost your damn mind, Jackie? You just kissed the mother of my child right in front of my face. Jackie, that's some disrespectful shit."

"Get over yourself, Eric. I haven't been happy in a long time. Megan, I would really like it if you could put on your bathing suit so we could go swimming. I remember watching you, Kim and Ashley swim in the family pond."

"Sounds like a plan, Jackie."

"Megan, could you wear the hot pink swimsuit? Megan, you really do look amazing when you rock that little number."

"Jackie, I would like a word with you in the family room. Jackie, you sure are acting crazy today, woman."

"Eric, whatever, you're always acting crazy. Listen, Eric, I really don't have time to talk, me and Megan just made plans. Eric, why don't you go spend time with baby Maya and get to know her."

"Jackie, you're really showing your ass right now. Megan, I'll meet you at the pond."

Before Jackie left, she planted a soft kiss on my forehead. I already knew it was gonna be some shit when Eric got left behind.

"Megan, what in the hell have you done to my wife?"

"I promise you, Eric, I didn't do anything. Jackie seduced me. I'm still in shock."

"I really can't blame my wife for falling for you. Megan, do you really want to spend time with Jackie?"

"I guess, Eric."

"Jackie needs some special attention. Megan, I have two thousand, all for you. Make sure my wife enjoys herself at the pond. Megan, after you've finished with my wife, meet me at my private room. Is that understood, beautiful?"

As I approached the pond, Jackie was already waiting for me, butterball naked. While I was completely grossed out to witness a middle-aged woman naked and horny, I also started feeling sorry for her at the same time. Jackie didn't waste any time trying to explore and kiss all over my body. Once Jackie found what she was looking for, she ate my box for at least an hour. Jackie's ass was so satisfied, we laid on the grass in silence.

Just like clockwork, Eric was waiting passionately in our private room.

"Damn, Megan, why did it have to take you so long to seduce my wife? What were y'all doing outside, making love?"

"Eric, Jackie's got a lot of pent-up frustration she's dealing with."

Just as Eric was about to kiss me on my mouth, Jackie un-apologetically walked into the room. Eric was looking at Jackie like she lost her damn mind.

"Jackie, what in the hell is your problem now?"

"Eric, I'm making the rules at this time. Megan isn't just your woman, she's my woman too, and from now on, we're all a couple. Listen up, Eric. Tomorrow night, all of us will sleep together in our main bedroom. Eric, when my brother and his family arrive at our home, I'll inform him that me and you decided to have an open marriage which includes the mother of your child. I don't want to feel like I'm hiding anything from him because you know how nosy Thomas can get. I know you're shocked, Eric, with my demands. Eric, you're just gonna have to deal with me falling in love with Megan. Anyway, you two, let's go to bed. Thomas and his family will be arriving at eight in the morning."

"Jackie, I'm confused, who will I sleep by?"

"Megan, you will sleep in the middle, silly. Baby girl, don't worry about your clothes or anything, the maids will be moving all of your belongings into our bedroom. I think for now, we're all gonna enjoy our new arrangement. Eric, just think, we don't have to sneak around and try to lay up with Megan."

Chapter Nine

"Ashley, I got a plan for us to make extra money."

"What is it now, Kim I'm getting tired of your side-job ideas."

"Whatever, you lazy bitch. Ashley, you shouldn't be complaining. You have two kids here that are always needy and growing out of some shit. Ashley, I think when you're not tricking, you can start selling dinners."

"Selling dinners does sound like a plan, Kim. Maybe our neighbors next door would love a home-cooked meal?"

"Girl, fuck their dope-slanging ass. I don't want to get caught up in nothing they got going on. Ashley, I forgot to tell you that we both have dates in about an hour, so go wash your box."

"Kim, thanks for the heads up, bitch."

"No problem, bitch."

"Kim, I need to chill out in the backyard before this stranger shows up."

"Don't get robbed, we do live by a bunch of sketchy folks."

Damn, I can't tell Kim the real reason I was going to the backyard. Once I laid my eyes on the nice-sized package of cocaine, my mouth started watering. As soon as I had the coke in my possession, I got scared and ran in the house, up the stairs, so I could get high as a kite.

Every time I get high, I'm always thinking about Stud's father and how we got to messing around with each other. It's a damn shame my own father wasn't even dead for a month good before Momma came in my room and announced that she had just gotten married. Momma had the nerve to tell me that I wasn't invited because she didn't have extra money to buy me a dress, and she didn't want me coming to the reception looking bummy.

In the beginning, my new father wouldn't open up his mouth to say one word to me. Then one day, everything changed. I heard my new father and mother arguing one night. My stepfather informed my mother that her coochie was musty. While waiting for my parents to stop arguing, I went downstairs to make some cookies from scratch. While walking into the kitchen, I ran into my stepfather pacing back and forth, whispering to himself, "Why did I marry this cunt?"

I guess I startled him because when he saw me, he rolled his eyes. "Sorry, Poppa, I didn't know you were in the kitchen."

"Kid, I'm not your father, and I wouldn't ever want to be. Little girl, next time address me as 'Mister.' Do I make myself clear?"

"Yes, sir."

"How old are you now, Ashley?"

"I just turned fifteen a week ago."

"Why didn't your mammy inform me that your birthday passed?"

"Momma didn't want me to make a big deal about my birthday, plus money was tight, Mister, y'all just had gotten married."

"Ashley, I don't have a lot of money, but here's twenty dollars. Go buy you a dress or something."

I was so happy. Nobody had given me more than five dollars in my life, and if they tried, Momma would take it and put it in her bra and say it was hers.

"Thanks, Poppa, I mean, Mister."

As I was about to turn around, Mister made sure to tell me how my butt looked in my pajamas. "Ashley, you keep wearing them shorts, I'm gonna put something in there, girl."

The crazy thing was, I was kinda flattered by Mister in a weird, crazy way. I looked back at my stepfather and batted my eyes suddenly, and when I walked away, I made sure to give Mister a little show. Ever since my weird interaction with Mister, it seemed like he started to crush on me more and more. Mister would make sure to tell me how fine I was and how I smelled like roses. Everything really got out of control at my house. I started enjoying Mister's kind words. Before I knew it, my mother's husband made me into a woman.

As usual, Momma was pissed at Mister because he quit three jobs in less than a month.

"I'm so tired of your sorry unemployed ass, Michael. I have to work two jobs, and you can't keep one."

"I can't keep my job because you're constantly stressing me out. You can't cook, you're fucking lazy in the bedroom, and your pussy has an odor to it."

While they argued for another hour, I heard my mother slamming the front door. All the arguing, I forgot Momma had to go to work. While my parents were arguing, I had whipped myself up a little potato salad and fried chicken. My real father taught me how to cook before he died. Before I knew it, Mister came in the kitchen, butterball naked, and sat at the table, while asking where was his food, because he was hungry.

I was so shocked by his nonchalant attitude. I couldn't believe that my mother's husband was sitting at our dinner table naked. I had never seen any man without clothes on, and here my stepfather was exposing himself to me.

"Mister, where are your clothes? If Momma comes back and sees you without no clothes on talking to me, she'll kill both of us."

"Fuck your old-ass momma, I'm hungry. Fix me something to eat, baby girl. I've been waiting for you to get done cooking."

While fixing Mister his plate, he grabbed me and made me sit on his lap. "I want you to feed me?" While feeding Mister, Mister took some of the potato salad and placed it on his penis.

"I see you haven't eaten anything yet, Ashley? Mister, I'm a virgin. I'm not ready for this, Mister."

"Ashley, it seems like you're ready, you're feeding me and got your ass on my leg. Ashley, what would your mother say if I informed her that you were enticing me? Ashley, be a good girl who sucks potato salad off my dick.”

I was hungry. I had been up here for hours. I don't know if I'm able to do this. While Mister guided me toward his penis, he made sure I sucked his penis until he came. While I was supposed to feel nasty, I was enjoying every bit of Mister's large penis. Mister ripped off my clothes and bent me over and started humping me in my butt. I screamed so loud, I'm sure our neighbor heard everything. Then, after he ripped my body a new one, he entered my vagina and demanded that I call him "Daddy."

After all of that, while Mister's love started to feel amazing, we made love two more times that night. That was my first encounter with my stepfather. I hated to think it but I was a better wife to Mister than Momma could ever be. Momma truly had competition. I was his wife when Momma wasn't around.

While still in my thoughts, Tara and Toya's fast ass had to interrupt my thoughts.

“Momma, we hungry. You been upstairs for hours.”

“I'll be downstairs in a minute. Y'all stay hungry. Y'all better learn how to cook.”

Chapter Ten

"Momma, it's a party happening downtown. Can we go?"

"Girl, I really ain't in no mood to be hanging downtown, partying nowhere. Momma, ain't you tired of sitting here looking at these four walls? Aunty Kim said that she didn't mind going either. I guess. I don't wanna stay all day."

"Okay Momma, I'll go tell Aunty Kim and Toya that you said we were going to the party."

As we were leaving, I could have sworn that I saw Bill's shadow. This can't be right, my imagination was fucking with me. Wow, I'm glad I decided to come out. Everybody seemed to be enjoying themselves. There was a bunch of people doing the Electric Slide, drinking, laughing, partying like rockstars. The strangest thing was I couldn't kick the thought of someone still watching us. Damn, I shouldn't have snorted that line of coke before we left.

The day was going great. The Thomas Brothers were playing in the background. I even snuck off to go do another round of cocaine. Yeah, I was feeling my cheerios now that I was high as a kite. Just as I was about to sneak back to the party, Kim startled the shit out of me.

"Hey, Ashley, what's your no good, why are you hiding back here?"

"I just needed time to myself for a minute."

"What the hell is on your nose, Ashley?"

Damn, I musta forgot to wipe the coke residue off my nose. "Girl, I freshened up with baby powder and I must have gotten some of it on my face."

"Bitch, that ain't no baby powder, that's cocaine you got on your nose. When did you pick that disgusting habit up?"

"It's not a big deal, Kim. I only been snorting coke for about a couple of weeks now. Kim, it's not like I'm addicted or anything."

"Bitch, you're gonna have to stop fucking with that garbage before you become a fully addicted cokehead. Anyway, it's time to go, we have two dates a piece that we're entertaining together."

While pulling into our driveway, I could've sworn that I saw someone's shadow appear by our blinds. As soon as we walked into our blacked-out home, someone jumped me and Kim from the back.

All I could remember was falling to the floor. Someone started kicking me in my head and shouting at us to get our stanking asses up off the floor. As I tried to get my thoughts together, I yelled out for my girls, and they didn't answer me. Kim was right beside me with blood gushing out of her mouth. I had blood leaking from my nose, and my mouth was burning from our abductor kicking me in my face. Before I could ask again where my girls were, Bill's nasty ass ran up on Kim and punched her in the face. Then he punched me in the face as well. I didn't even notice the four other men that accompanied Bill.

"Since y'all wanna play with me and act like children, I'm a treat y'all like kids."

Once again, the man started kicking our ass. It was two men fighting me, and the other man was on top of Kim while Bill watched us get fucked up. Just when I thought Bill's goons was done fucking us up, they had the nerve to start whipping us with stitching cords. That's when I blacked all the way the fuck out.

I didn't know if it was the coke or the ass-whipping, but I started to have flashbacks of when Momma beat me with a stitching cord for flirting with my Mister. While I thought Momma was taking a quick nap, I forgot my drying towel in the room. I didn't know

Momma's new husband had came out the room, only for him to catch me sneaking into my room butterball naked.

"Nice pair of breasts you got, girl, and that ass is getting fatter day by day."

I tried not to laugh at his corny comment. Instead, I bent over un-apologetically to pick up my son's basketball and to show him what I really was working with. Just when I thought I was too cute, Momma came out of nowhere and ran up on me and punched me in my head. As dazed as I was, I knew that I was gonna get my ass beat for showing out in front of my new father. All I heard my mother saying repeatedly was that I was a piece of shit. Momma grabbed two stitching cords and she whooped my ass until blood was gushing from my body.

"Now get your stank ass up and don't ever let me catch you flirting with my man, Bitch. Bitch, stop all that crying before you wake Stud's crybaby ass up. Ashley, this is your warning, Bitch. I'll kill you if I catch you taunting my man again."

Just as if Momma didn't warn me, me and my new stepfather started having an affair a week later. Damn, I got some good pussy. I just couldn't keep my mother's husband off me. When I felt the stitching cord hit my face, that's when I woke all the way up, and I felt someone pick me up off the floor and dump my limped body in the trunk. I wasn't alone, Kim was badly beat up and knocked out. I could hear the men talking loudly in the background, talking about "we just got a workout of beating them two bitches' asses." Then one of the men bragged about how much money they pocketed from our beat-down. Once the car stopped, that's when I got scared all over again. "Oh my God, did Bill pay his goons to murder us also? Dear God, please don't let Bill harm my girls. I know I haven't been a good mother, but I promise you, Lord, I will change."

All of a sudden, the creepy guys opened the trunk. Shit happened so quick. The three goons that beat our ass grabbed us out of the truck and threw us on the concrete, but not just any concrete. We were back at our old stomping grounds. The place where Kim and I ran off and left our babies at. Damn, how am I gonna face my son knowing that I abandoned him? What type of sick person runs out on their baby? That's when I heard my girls asking me and Kim if we were okay. I think Kim was still dazed by the left hook Bill landed on her face.

"Momma, are you alright? Bill sent us outside to check on you and Kim, and from the looks of things, you and Aunty Kim lost that round."

"Girl, get your fast ass away from me. We got jumped by some hood dudes, and that's the only reason we're fucked up. Bill told me to tell y'all that we still have to stay in the cottage. Bill also got really annoying and informed me that our old home is in need of a good old-fashioned cleaning. Toya, I don't know how he wants me to clean when I think my arm is broken. The bastards done fucked up my arm, and now I got to do manual labor."

Chapter Eleven

"Eric, I can't believe your wife is letting your whore stay right here under your roof?"

"Michael, I'm the man in my household. Michael, I run shit. Actually, Megan belongs to me and Jackie. Megan is our woman."

"Eric, you mean to tell me you and Jackie both take turns fucking your baby's mother? We are enjoying her company. I never felt so satisfied. Eric, you're gonna have to let me tap that before me and my family head back home."

"That's up to Jackie, she's gotten really protective of that pussy lately."

"Eric King, let me inform you about your hard-headed ass son? Bill has brought back his dog-ass baby mommas. Them beat-up cunts is laying up our cottage as we speak. Kim and her for-the-street-ass maid ain't thought about my grandkids in months, and they really think that they're gonna just come back like shit is sweet?"

"Jackie, just calm down and let Bill handle his family."

"Mr. and Mrs. King, you have a guest."

"Who is it, Randall?"

"The woman at the door said she was Megan's mother."

"Randall, escort Megan's mother to the back entrance. I don't want nobody we know to catch her filthy ass on my property. Michael, before we meet Megan's trashy mother, I'm just gonna tell you only one time, if I catch your eyeballs in the same direction as Megan's, I will personally cut off your manhood."

"No need to act like a bitch, Sis. Jackie, I just wanted a little sample of Megan before we head back home. Jackie, you really are a selfish bitch. You know I'm a faithful man. You heard what I said, little brother. About time myself and Eric made it to our study to meet Megan's mother, that bitch already made herself comfortable. Megan's mother had the nerve to have her stank ass literally laying on my desk. I had to gather this simple bitch all the way together. Get your crazy ass off my desk. We do have chairs you can sit on."

"Whatever, Jackie, I would rather be sitting on Eric's face, or your face, either or."

I couldn't believe this scallywag was sitting in my home talking to me and my husband crazy. Eric's ass was just standing there like he was stuck on stupid.

"What is this meeting about? Myself or my husband? We don't have time to be chilling with your welfare-looking ass."

"Jackie, let's keep shit real cute before I expose you perverts for being super freaks on the low, and I don't know if you know this, but you have bloody females laying on your lawn."

"Brenda, how much money will it take for you to keep your fucking mouth closed?"

"A lot, Bitch, and I will let you know when and how much, but for now, I'll be needing a place to stay and my own maid."

"That sounds like a plan, we have a small house about an hour away from here."

"Jackie, that's too far away from my daughter and granddaughter. I'm gonna remind y'all motherfuckers about life. Y'all don't get to fuck on my daughter and keep my only grandchild away from me. I was thinking about staying real close, like right here."

"Bitch, you ain't staying your filthy ass in my house."

"Jackie, I'm tired of talking to you. Get my room together before I start running my motherfucking mouth. Y'all some nasty, ungrateful motherfuckers. My husband and I gave y'all our only daughter to fuck on, and you don't know how to treat her mother. Oh, Jackie, and tell your little male maid that I would like a cocktail A.S.A.P."

Chapter Twelve

Damn. This shit is really startin' to feel like a job. I have to wake up, feed Mia, love on her, then fuck on Eric and Jackie for a few hours. Damn, I'm really startin' to get tired of all this silly shit.

While I was stuck in my thoughts, I heard some moanin' and groanin' sounds comin' from next to my room. I started to get jealous because, who the fuck is fuckin' on my tricks? So I looked in the peephole and got a rude awakening. Jackie's brother, Michael, was fuckin' my momma doggy style. I almost pissed on myself.

First of all, how dare Momma sneak back here, knowin' good and well Jackie gonna be callin' the cops. Even though me and Momma wasn't close, I still didn't wanna see her locked up for trespassin'. Before I knew it, I opened the door and started yellin' at Momma to put her clothes on. They had the nerve to ignore me like I wasn't even talkin'. Momma's triflin' ass wouldn't stop suckin' Michael's dick to save her life.

Michael yelled out that he had a two-for-one special. I guess he thought I was gonna join his cheatin' ass. Damn shame his wife and children were right downstairs. "Momma, you have to get the fuck out of here before Jackie walks in and calls the cops!"

As if "cops" was the magic word to stop Momma from deep-throatin' Michael. "Megan, you sure are a hatin'-ass little bitch. Oh, Jackie didn't inform you that we are roommates now?"

"Momma, how did you get Jackie to agree to let you stay here?"

"I blackmailed that bitch. Jackie's ass better fall in line 'cause she knows I'm the one she needs to worry about. Oh, Michael, before you leave, run me my motherfuckin' pocket change."

"Momma, you really are somethin' else. How dare you come to my home and start punkin' bitches?"

"Megan, watch your motherfuckin' tone before I two-piece your ass. I'll put hands and feet on your punk ass. Remember, bitch, you came out of my pussy. Keep runnin' your mouth, bitch, I promise you I'll knock you the fuck out."

"Momma, that's why I don't want you stayin' here, 'cause you violent."

"Megan, I'm not the one that's violent, Bill is. Megan, you didn't see them two beat-up bitches that was stretched out on the lawn?"

"No, I didn't realize we had company."

"Megan, Bill done fucked them hoes up. Bill got them two bitches swolled up for months."

"Momma, you don't understand. Bill has finally found his wife and his baby mother. Momma, they ran away months ago. I better go check on my friends."

"Oh, you must be a better bitch, Megan? You got friends all of a sudden?"

"Yes, Momma, they *my* friends. More like family. Somethin' you know nothin' about."

While walkin' away from Momma, all I could think about was my biological grandmother. Up until I was twelve, I stayed with my grandmother, who loved and treated me with respect. One day, I heard my grandmother arguin' with a young couple who kept insistin' that they were my real parents and that they had permission from the state to come get me. I had never seen any pictures or heard any chatter about my parents, so I always thought they didn't want me. "Hurry up and get my child's shit packed up, you old bat!"

I had a weird flashback to the time Momma and Pappa made me go without food for two days because I didn't want to fuck everybody's community preacher. All I could remember was Mr. Tom lookin' at me through his thick bifocals, wishin' and hopin' that one day he would get the chance to get between my legs.

One sunny day, me and my family was walkin' by the church, and I guess Mr. Thomas started smilin' and kinda foamin' at the mouth when he laid eyes on me. Momma must have sensed his fucked-up attraction, and Daddy instantly saw huge dollar signs. Instantly, Momma and Daddy got right to the point. "Hey, piece of shit, would you like to smell my teenage daughter's pussy for a few hundred dollars?"

Pastor Thomas was so caught off guard by my parents' words that he quietly said, "I'll pay top dollar." My Daddy looked like he just won the lottery. Pastor Tom gave Daddy five hundred dollars to spend the whole night with me. I was so scared. My parents' crazy asses let him just take me home without even sayin' goodbye.

The car ride to Pastor Tom's house was long, and he wouldn't even say a word. But shit changed real quick. Pastor Tom turned into an animal. He started referrin' to me as a devil child, never used my real name. The bastard had the nerve to say, since he was touched with God's special hands, that he was gonna save me from my evil, whorish ways.

Before I knew it, I drop-kicked Pastor Tom in his face. Blood sprayed everywhere. I knew from my behavior, Daddy was gonna put hands on me. It didn't take long before my father found out about my drop-kick. Pappa sent Momma to finish up the job I done fucked up. Pastor Tom took back a hundred dollars of his money because he said Momma was old and tired. Pappa punished me by starvin' me for two whole days, and on top of that, he beat my ass good and proper.

Chapter Thirteen

As I knelt down to wipe the blood off my best friend, Ashley, I couldn't help but be concerned about Kim. Where was she? Did Bill murder Kim and remove the body? While I was in my thoughts, waiting for Ashley to wake up, Toya whispered very softly, "Megan, will Momma recover from the beatdown?"

"I don't want y'all to worry about your mother. I'll take good care of her. I want you to go to the big house and get some bandages, some alcohol, oh, and don't forget to grab the Tylenol out of the medicine cabinet. Ashley will need the whole damn bottle of Tylenol after the ass-whooping she endured."

"What the fuck, is this a dream? Am I dreaming? I got my ass whooped by three of Bill's goons and can't see out of both eyes because them bum bastards punched me like cowards, and now someone is fucking me doggy style from the back. Motherfucker, slow down. I ain't going nowhere. I know I still got blood gushing from my body, and your dirty ass still wanna fuck?" My body was getting abused by Bill. Bill must have wanted me to suffer, because as soon as he was done violating me, he started to suffocate me with a pillow.

Oh, my God, I never would have imagined that Bill would be suffocating me and that I would be meeting my maker soon. I remember when we were both madly in love with each other. Bill promised me that he would love and take care of me forever, and now he's trying to take my life. While in and out of consciousness, I started dreaming about the first time I met Bill.

I had just graduated high school with all A's. My parents promised me that if I got all A's in school, they would send me to Paris. I always dreamed of living there and marrying a nice rich man from Paris. I was born in New Orleans with both my parents being proud Creoles. One thing about my parents, they didn't take shit from anybody. To be honest, my parents were known to be uppity Black folks who didn't mind reminding a few haters that they didn't have the same ancestry. Not only did my parents think they were better than their own race, they thought they were better than white folks too. Momma would always say, "They got all that money and good schooling, and their lazy asses only speak one language." My parents were fluent in French, Spanish, and sign language for the deaf.

I was the only child of my mother and father. My father was married before and had three sons from his first wife. Momma was extremely jealous of his first family. The minute Momma got Daddy to marry her, she made my father move far away from his offspring.

I will always remember the day Daddy came home all excited and announced that I would be getting married in the morning to an African American billionaire by the name of Bill King. Of course, I was beside myself.

"Daddy, I'm not marrying no total stranger. I'm going to Paris for college, you promised. I'm definitely not marrying no colored guy. Daddy, I thought you said that the colors were lazy bastards?"

Before I knew it, Daddy slapped me clean across the room. "Listen, little girl, Bill doesn't have a color that's attached to him. Bill is a billionaire, and he already paid top dollar for you. Kim, go put your fucking girl dress on. Kim, you will be having dinner today in the next hour."

I was so pissed. Daddy never raised a hand to me before. While applying makeup to my bruised face, all I could think about was marrying a complete stranger and missing out on going to Paris for the summer.

As soon as I heard my father's voice, my ass jumped up. "Kim, hurry up and get downstairs. Bill King is waiting for you at the dinner table." My father better be lucky I'm scared of his ass because I would have told him to go straight to hell. "Damn, I forgot I had a date with this fine ass heffa up the street from me."

While walking into my dining room, I could already tell by my future husband's face that he was with the shit. Bill gave me a look that made me feel like he knew that I was also with the same shit. Bill quietly interrupted my father when he tried to introduce us.

"Listen, Sir, I don't mean no harm or disrespect. I don't have time to make small talk. I paid you big money, and it's time for me and Kim to be getting married and leaving. Oh, don't worry about clothes, my maid will pick you up some new garments."

"You mean I'm leaving right now?"

"Yes, beautiful, I have to get back home soon. I'm a very busy man."

"Where is Momma?"

"She's in the living room with the Priest."

"Daddy, y'all really are serious about me marrying a complete stranger?"

"Listen, Kim, be a good girl and please don't make Bill King regret giving me all this money. Stop getting all in your feelings, Kim. I didn't know your mother at all when I married her. Kim, please make me and your mother proud, at least until the check

clears."

Chapter Fourteen

"Bill, I know your black ass didn't just bring them cunts back to my house? My maid informed me that there was a bloody mess leading all the way to my cottage."

"I thought you gave me the cottage, Momma?"

"Don't get smart, asshole. Bill, who the fuck gave you some authority to bring them animals back to my home? My grandsons don't need them funky cunts around. Ain't no telling what kind of nasty virus they picked up."

"Momma, you really are crazier than a busy bug if you thought that I was gonna take care of some bastard babies. Mom, you seem to have fallen in love with them little mistakes. I still don't give three fucks about either one of those hoes' kids."

"Bill, what in the hell are you gonna do with your women?"

"I plan on slavin' them hoes until I get tired, and hopefully they'll take their whore asses somewhere else and find themself a new family. Momma, I already got a few jobs planned for them raggedy hoes."

"Just keep your trashy bitches away from the big house. Bill, I don't want them musty hoes near my gate."

"Don't worry, Momma, I'm 'bout to work them hoes."

"Bill, I forgot to tell you that Amanda and the boys will be coming tomorrow." Just before Bill could respond, I knew it was my exit. I knew Bill would be on fire. He sure didn't want to see Amanda. Amanda was coming to get in his pockets. That's what that sorry motherfucker gets for bringing them hoes back on my land.

"Momma, it's time for you to wake up now. Bill brought your yelling baby over here an hour ago. Corey hasn't stopped crying at all."

"Aunt Megan told me to tell you that she'll be back. She had to breastfeed baby Mya."

"Toya, I feel like someone ran me over with a Mack truck. I needed some coke so bad, just to knock the edge off."

While trying to get up so I could deal with my crying baby, I started smelling Bill's over-the-top cologne. Before I knew it, Bill punched me right in the face, right in front of my children. Me and my girls stood there in horror.

"Toya, Tara, the maids can use y'all's help at the big house."

My kids ran off out of fear that Bill would tear their face up too.

"Don't talk or breathe, bitch. You really fucked with the wrong motherfucker."

As Bill was about to reach for my neck, I heard Megan in the background begging Bill to leave me alone. As if Megan's voice was what Bill needed to stop him from fucking me up. "What are you doing here, you noisy bitch?"

"Bill, you already beat her up once. She can't take no more ass-kicking."

"Fuck that slave. Anyways, slave, I'm gonna be putting your dirty ass to work. I need you to clean up the horse shit in the barn. When you're finished with that, slave, the pigs got shit everywhere outside. Ashley, when you're done with those two tasks, come see me. I'll find you some more work. Megan, mind your business next time. Megan, check me out later tonight. I would love for you to suck the cum off my dick again."

"I'll do whatever you want, Bill, just please don't hit Ashley again."

"Ashley, get your dog ass out of my sight. You have plenty of odd jobs to do today. Megan, get on your knees, hoe. I want my dick to be sucked right now."

Bill shoved Ashley out the cottage and pushed me down on the floor. I knew what I had to do. I didn't mind, though. I was built for the abuse.

Chapter Fifteen

After my encounter with Bill, I was on a mission to find Kim. Just as I was about to walk out of the cottage, Kim was walking in.

"Kim, I was so worried about you. You look horrible, Kim."

"Megan, Bill hired three big cock diesel dudes to fuck us up. Megan, where is Ashley? Bill gave her some chores to do. Megan, that motherfucker is bat-shit crazy. Bill just got done raping me doggy style. I swear, Megan, if I had a gun, I would've sent that motherfucker to his maker. Since y'all been gone, he started putting his big dick inside me."

"Kim, I missed you guys so much. What have y'all been up to for all these months?"

"Girl, we've been on some pimp shit. Lovin' them and leavin' them punk-ass men. Megan, we were receiving money from everybody. Bitch, I even tricked with a preacher. Megan, this motherfucker preached even when I was giving him some of my fire head. That motherfucker told me that I was going straight to heaven."

Just as I was about to tell Megan another one of our adventures, something funkier than a motherfucker passed my nose. It was Ashley, covered in pig, cow, and horse shit.

"Damn, bitch, is that you, smelling like a fucking stank animal?"

"Yes, bitch, Bill made me clean up all the farm animal's shit."

"That low-down dirty motherfucker. Bill rapes me, he has you cleaning up shit. That dog-ass motherfucker will pay for how he treated us. Y'all, let's go jump in the pond buck naked like we used to, because my body is so sore I could use some relaxation."

"Ashley, please bring you some soap, because your funky ass is starting to give me a headache."

Just as we were about to jump in the pond, my mother emerged out of the water like she was some sort of fish. Of course, Momma was buck naked also. "Hey, you little ugly ducklings, it looks like you are in need of some good girl time?"

"Megan, who the fuck is this new bitch swimming in my pond? Megan, you better get that beaten-up bitch all the way together before I redot that bitch's eyeball."

"You better watch your mouth, little bitch, or I'll go get Bill and make him fuck you up one more time."

"Enough, Momma, these women are my friends."

"Megan, this homely-looking bitch is your mother?"

"Yeah, she's the one that birthed me. I didn't get a chance to tell you that Jackie is letting my mother stay here for a spell."

"I hope it's a short spell, because I already know that I don't like your mother at all."

"Megan, I'll see you at the big house. I got to get from around these cunts before I put my hands around your little friends' throats. Please don't think shit is sweet, bitch. I got my razor hidden in my pussy. I will cut your ass from your front to your back."

"Calm down, Momma, ain't nobody putting their hands on anybody."

"Well, good. Since I don't have to fuck one of you bitches up, it's time for me to get higher than a kite."

As if cocaine was the magic word, my frown definitely turned into a smile. I tried to kick my cocaine habit ever since I got home. When Megan's mom mentioned getting high, I started to feel a sudden rush of enjoyment. While we relaxed in our favorite hideaway pond, we started gossiping about how Momma snuck in the big house and how Jackie and her bat-shit crazy family members had been running a train on me since y'all ran away.

"Megan, I knew Bill's crusty ass was gonna be trying to fuck. Megan, let me find out Jackie likes pussy?"

"Shit, her old ass munched on my box like she had something to prove." With that being said, we busted out laughing.

"Oh, I forgot to tell y'all that they're opening up a new club called the Breakwall. It's right next door to the hotel. Megan, do you remember when we took those bitches' boyfriends? I was so drunk. Girl, all I can remember is his big black dick hanging out of my mouth."

"I'm wondering will Tory Long have his stank ass there performing. Tory better not be there, fucking loser. He has abandoned his own flesh and blood."

"Bitch, didn't you tell my son the same story?"

"Fuck your punk-ass son. Fuck them runaway bastards."

"Ashley, let's stop talking about Kim's baby daddies before she gets in her feelings. Anyway, are y'all going out with me tonight?"

"Bitch, I don't want Bill to fuck me up again."

"Bitch, make me understand how you scared of my husband? Bill better leave us the fuck alone. We came back to our brats just like he demanded."

As we were leaving our private pond, we noticed Amanda, her baby, and her two little brothers camped out on the front lawn like they owned the joint.

"Why the fuck is this dog-ass bitch back here bothering me? Damn, that bitch done had a whole baby and she's still shaped like a little boy. Oh, bad body-ass bitch. Fucking corny-ass bitch went behind my back and fucked on Stud."

"Kim, I understand that you're in your feelings, but I have to go. I have a double date with Jackie and Eric.

"Megan, be on time because we're leaving to go out around nine o'clock, and we will leave your two-timing ass."

"Kim, don't worry, I'm sit on both of their faces and ride their old ass off to sleep."

Chapter Sixteen

"Grandma, what's been going on since I've been gone? There's a scary lady in the kitchen cussing out everybody. Grandma, she even had the nerve to tell me to stay the fuck out of her way. I'll have to explain later, Amanda, it's a long story."

"Grandma, I'm scared. She looks like she's trained to go."

"I'll go calm our guest down. Amanda, the crazy lady is Megan's mother. I invited her to stay here for a spell."

"Grandma, are you serious? That woman is crazy. I can see all her craziness from her bitch-ass eyes."

"Like I said, Amanda, she will be staying here for a spell. Just keep out of her way."

"One of y'all maids done stole my dope? I know y'all thieving asses done ran off with my dope. I'm only gonna ask y'all motherfuckers once before I start to put my hands around each of your necks. Unleash my crack, bitches! Where the fuck is my fucking medicine, whores?"

"Tonya, calm your crazy ass down talking to my staff like that."

"Jackie, you better get these motherfucking thieves. One of them stole my crack."

"Tonya, I will kick your nothing ass out. I know you didn't bring drugs into my home? There are young babies staying here. Don't get beside yourself, Tonya. I'll call 911 and your crackhead ass will be locked up before you know it."

"Jackie, fuck you. You're a nasty bitch. If I'm to be locked up, I'm taking you and your entire nasty-ass family with me. I'm gonna be sure to call the law and happily inform them that you, your husband, and son enjoy licking my daughter's ass every day. Jackie, you got the nerve to be in my face about a whorehouse. Y'all motherfuckers got all the hoes, guns, and the drugs in this legal whorehouse. Bitch, all of you nasty motherfuckers have raped my daughter repeatedly."

"Tonya, if you can calm your crazy ass down, I will find someone to replace your drugs."

"That's what I thought, bitch. Run and get my crack before I start running my motherfucking mouth. Oh, and tell your granddaughter that I don't give a fuck how young she is. I will put my foot in her ass."

"Tonya, calm down."

"Bitch, run me my motherfucking crack. Bitch, I'm grown as fuck, don't ever tell me to calm down. Matter of fact, Jackie, go play in Megan's ass and talk to her like a child. Jackie, when I find out which one of your maids stole my shit, I'm still fucking their ass up."

After the long, drawn-out argument with Megan's mother, all I could think about was Megan sitting on my face. I couldn't believe how pussy-whipped I really was. How could my husband's whore have me willing to do anything to keep her in my house? The shit I have to go through for pleasure. Fuck it, if I have to deal with Megan's crackhead mother for a spell, then so be it.

I realized that I needed Megan's good loving as I walked into my room. Eric's cheating ass was already fucking on Megan. Megan was riding my husband's face repeatedly. Once I finally joined them, I was beyond pissed off. Fuck, they were already sweaty and funky from fucking. When Megan noticed my displeasure, she patiently told me to lay down so I could taste some of her juices.

"I hope you're not mad, Jackie? You was taking so long."

"I was in the kitchen calming down your mother." As if knowing what I wanted, Megan put her whole ass in my mouth. Megan started massaging Eric's penis until he came. Megan was so amazing that I forgot about her mother, and I also forgot about how my husband stayed trying to get more pussy behind my back.

"Amanda, come get your spoiled-ass baby. I already informed your mother when y'all came that my servants aren't your babysitters."

"Dad, I just went to the bathroom."

"Next time, take that hollering-ass child right along with you while you're pissing."

"Dad, why doesn't anybody say anything when Megan leaves her baby with the house staff?"

"Because she's your grandparent's whore, that's why! Listen up, Amanda, I am not going back and forth with my own child. Just keep that little crybaby away from me. I already can't stand when y'all come and visit."

"We didn't even wanna come. Momma made us come to this crazy house."

Before I knew it, Daddy slapped me so hard I flew on the ground. "Amanda, you better never come to my home acting like you're somebody. And the next time you talk to me about how your trifling mammy tricked me into keeping y'all's little demon seeds, I'm gonna put my foot dead in your ass. I should have been whooping your ass for the old and the new. Now get yourself cleaned up and watch how you talk to me."

"Stud, it's not safe for you to come back here."

"Momma, I have nowhere else to go. I've been sleeping on the streets for two weeks. Grandma kicked me out and had the nerve to throw my clothes out the window and told me to fetch it. Grandma got mad at me because I refused to give her my last couple of dollars. I told Grandma I would give her money next week. Momma, her old ass lost her mind. Momma, Grandma literally told me to kick rocks. I need for you to hide me out until I can find somewhere else to go."

"Stud, you're gonna get me fucked up by Bill."

"Momma, I didn't come here to cause you any pain. I really need your help."

"I guess you can stay in the attic for a spell. Just don't draw attention to yourself."

"Momma, you have white shit on your nose? How long have you been sniffing coke?"

"None of your business, boy. Ask me again about shit that doesn't concern you and your ass will be getting out of here too. Stud, be careful. Kim still wants to fuck you up for walking away from the Bill Junior."

"Momma, I still don't know if that baby is even mine."

"Oh, I forgot to mention that Amanda and your son are staying at the big house for a spell. I'm gonna keep it a buck with you, Stud. If Bill catches you here, I'm gonna act like I didn't know you were even here."

"Momma, let me find out you still have feelings for that snack motherfucker?"

"Like I said, mind your business and don't let nobody know you've been gone or are hiding upstairs in the attic. Momma, where are you going? You have got your fucking girl clothes laid out."

"Me, Kim, and Meagan are going out to shake a tail feather."

"Momma, how has Bill Junior and Corey been since I've been gone?"

"Shit, I don't know, I was on my bullshit. Me and Kim ghosted them bastards and tried to find peace in another state. Bill found out where we were located and beat our asses for the old and the new. Them punk motherfuckers got me good. Bill's goons had my whole body on swell."

Chapter Seventeen

"Damn, it's some sexy-ass men and women up in here. The DJ is playing my motherfucking song by Big Booty Judy. Every time 'Big Booty Judy's' song comes on the radio, I start shaking my ass in the mirror."

"Kim, you ain't got no rhythm, or no ass."

"Fuck you, Megan, you ain't nothing but a hating-ass hoe."

"Hey, sexy, can I buy you and your friends a round of drinks?"

"Sure, good lookin'. And how about afterwards you pay me five hundred for some fire-ass head and some of the best pussy in town?"

"How about I pay you a thousand?"

"You got a deal, good lookin'. I didn't catch your name, sweet thing?"

"My name is Megan, and my two good friends' names are Ashley and Kim."

"Hey, lover boy, if that cock is still working after I put this pussy on you, for an extra thousand you can run a train on all of us whores. We definitely got the best pussy around in New York."

"Damn, baby, you must be slumming for real. I ain't fucking with your pussy. Your husband Bill won't be looking for me with his pistol."

"Fuck Bill's hating ass. We definitely have an open marriage. So after you get done fucking on my friend, let me find out how that dick tastes."

After about ten vodka shots, we were all over the place, dancing on tables, humping on every single dick that amused us. Before long, we started stripping out of all our clothes. An hour later, Bill's associate decided to take each of us up on our offer. While I started sucking his dick, Megan sat on his face. Ashley's nasty ass started to suck on his toes. Ashley must have known some shit that we didn't, and before we knew it, our little trick was begging us to stop, but we didn't. We performed all kinds of sex acts on him, including sticking a dildo up his ass. We even spanked him with the very belt he was wearing. After our wild sexcapade, we left our trick divinely broke and with the dildo still hanging out of his ass.

"Bitch, hurry the fuck up. Damn, you ain't made me cum yet? What's wrong with your mouth? Have you been cheating on me? I... Amanda, you're starting to act like a lazy bitch?"

After rocking my cock back and forth in Amanda's mouth, I finally exploded. "Let me find out you been cheating on me? Stud, calm down."

"I haven't sucked or fucked nobody since we made love. Stud, it was too hard for me to get your twelve inches down my throat, that's all. We ain't gonna have time to fuck. My mom and her posse will be arriving in a minute."

"Amanda, make sure you keep me being here a secret. I don't want to fuck your father up."

"Stud, of course, it's a secret. We had all of this planned for months. We're gonna rob my family and take what belongs to me so we can really become a real family. Stud, with all the money that we're gonna take, we can move to another country and start over."

"Amanda, that shit sounds good. You better make good on your promise, because if your family finds out about our plan, I'm a dead man."

"Stud, we're supposed to be having a party tomorrow. We'll rob their ass blind and sneak off with our son."

"Bitch, it's time for you to kick rocks. I smell my mother and her crew a mile away."

Just as I was about to break my neck climbing out the attic window, I ran into Megan's scary-ass mother. "Look at the fleas on fluffy. What is your trifling ass doing outside at this time?"

"None of your fucking business, crackhead."

"Don't get fly, bitch. I'll inform your father that I caught you about to fall out the cabin's attic window, trying to be sneaky."

"What do you want, crackhead?"

"What do I want? I would like to sit my old pussy on your nice tender face. You really got me fucked up if you think that your disgusting pussy is going anywhere near my face."

"You was upstairs really slobbing on that young man's dick. You even tried to get that big horse down your throat. Maybe if you was a little nicer, I would teach you a couple of tricks. I also heard you telling that mandingo that y'all was gonna rob the house. Bitch, lay your tender ass down."

"I'm supposed to lay on the ground? Yeah, bitch, don't start acting like a better bitch now. Everyone knows you have loose legs."

In my wildest dreams, I never would have imagined some old crusty bitch would have her stank pussy in my mouth. This bitch was really raping the shit out of me. She started humping my face, then her old ass took her whole hand and started penetrating me. After being repeatedly raped by Megan's mother, I literally fainted while she was on top of me. I woke up without no clothes on, and I had a mouth full of cum in my mouth. Damn, I should've let that crackhead snitch on me. I couldn't risk getting Stud in trouble. Fuck, love got me getting raped by a crackhead.

Chapter Eighteen

"Kim, wake up! You have been summoned by Jackie to attend breakfast. Ashley, Mrs. King sent a list of chores you need to get done today. Mrs. King wanted me to inform you, Ashley, that you don't get privileges like everybody else."

"Bitch, get your 'marry the maid'-looking ass out of here. My girl Ashley knows that she has chores. Damn, I can't stand these new maids that Jackie hired. Bitches be running around this house dropping orders and shit."

"Kim, don't forget that we were gonna meet up with them freaks we met at the club."

"Ashley, you know that I'm always down to get into some bullshit."

"Kim, it's about time you arrived for breakfast. You should be grateful I'm allowing you to sit with me at my dinner table."

"I started not to come, Jackie, but I changed my mind. Jackie, you do know how I enjoy seeing y'all fake bitches?"

"Amanda, pass the eggs, you greedy bitch. Oh, Amanda, let me find out Bill dotted your eye? I know you were running your smart-ass mouth."

"Grandma, did we have to invite this trash for breakfast? I thought everything would be okay. It's my brother's last day here."

"Please, Amanda, let's not show out in front of my brother's wife."

"Jackie, this is some crazy shit that's happening right now? Jackie, why are we here pretending that we would ever like each other? Oh, your cum-sucking brother is upstairs fucking on Megan's mother."

While everyone froze up, I couldn't help but to start to laugh at their crazy asses. Before I knew it, Jackie backhanded me across the face. While slapping me one more good time in the face, her old ass gonna say how she missed putting her foot in my ass. Jackie's sister-in-law gonna scream out that she was glad somebody besides her had to suck his small-ass dick. Amanda's scary ass sucker punched me in the head and had the nerve to call me a punk-ass bitch.

Just like clockwork, Bill and Eric came to my rescue. Eric's crusty ass starts defending Jackie. "Kim, you're always antagonizing my wife. That's why my wife stay putting her foot in your ass."

"Eric, you better get this hating-ass bitch away from me! Y'all hating-ass rich bitches stay mad at me? I better not be leaking blood, you crusty-ass bitches."

"Eric, get that stank-trash bitch up out of my dining room before I black out on this bitch. I knew I shouldn't invite your bum ass, Kim. You still don't have any class, you're still a nothing-ass bitch."

After all that going back and forth, I managed to grab Amanda by her throat. It took Eric and Bill to remove my motherfucking hand from around Amanda's throat.

"Bitch, what the fuck are you doing in my room?"

"Ashley, it's been your dick-sucking ass that's been stealing all of my coke? Don't lie, bitch. I caught your thieving ass red-handed, you sneaking and geeking ass hoe. Run me my motherfucking dope, bitch."

Fuck, this bitch done caught me. And before I could run the fuck out of the room, Megan's mother dove on me like she was a football player. I didn't realize Megan's mother has that much strength.

"Damn, bitch, you're really tripping over some dope? Damn, I can't stand y'all stingy crackheads. Bitches hate to share anymore."

Before I knew it, Megan's mother kicked me in the head while I was still on the floor. Before she had a chance to kick me again, Megan ran in the room and literally shoved her mother away from me, almost knocking her to the ground.

"Megan, if you ever stick your dick-sucking fingertips on me again, I promise you I will send your bitch ass to your maker. I don't give a fuck if you're my child or not. I should've swallowed you, bitch."

"Momma, what the fuck are you fucking with Ashley for?"

"Your thieving-ass friend has been stealing my cocaine."

"Megan, I just borrowed a little bit of your mother's coke and she got all crazy on me. Fuck, I was gonna put her coke back, Megan. I was just waiting for Bill's stingy ass to lay his wallet down so I could replace her coke that I borrowed."

"Megan, get your dumb-ass friend the fuck out of my face before I put my hands on her again."

After all the ruckus and going back and forth with my mother, I knew that I had to check Ashley's crackhead ass about her new found addiction. "Ashley, you almost fell down a razor blade and ended up in an alcohol river. I want you to know that my mother doesn't mind going to jail over her dope. My mother is bat-shit crazy for real; she will pull a razor out of her mouth, or pussy, with the quickness. When the fuck did you start sneaking and geeking, Ashley?"

"Megan, I only fuck with dope on occasion, I'm not hooked or anything."

"Ashley, on some real shit, please leave that poison alone. I've been around a lot of people that got hooked on that poison so bad that they've sold their own kids. My parents done sold me so many times I've stopped counting."

Before we knew it, there was a loud commotion coming from downstairs. "Bitch, that could only be Mrs. Jackie and Kim beating the hell out of each other. Let's hurry up and get downstairs before Kim gets fucked up."

Once we got downstairs, it seemed like Eric had things under control. When Kim saw us coming, she started to turn up and tried to sucker punch Jackie. Bill must of sensed that Kim was gonna try to make a move. Bill put Kim's ass in a quick headlock so fast.

"Bill, I can't breathe, you musty-stank bastard. Get the fuck off my neck, you fucking women beater."

Bill started choking me even harder. The only reason he stopped was because someone rang the doorbell, and to all of our surprise, it was my mother and father. And if things couldn't have been weirder, Ashley's mother was with them.

Chapter Nineteen

"Kim, we're here to inform you that your trifling husband stopped paying the mortgage on the house, and now me and your mother are homeless."

"Damn, I knew I should've never trusted Bill's hood ass. Kim, why are you walking around your own house behaving like the maid?"

"Daddy, I've been living in hell. Bill lied about having money, this estate still belongs to his parents, and they hate my guts. And I just got jumped hood-style by Bill's mother, aunt, and his dog-ass daughter."

"Where's my grandson, Kim?"

"He's around here somewhere. Jackie tries to keep him away as much as possible. Jackie had the nerve to tell my son that I wasn't good enough to be around him. Daddy, you're gonna find out anyway. Bill has been having an affair with our maid and another woman that lives here with us."

"Did I just hear you say that my daughter has been sleeping with your husband?"

While I was complaining to my parents about my fucked-up marriage, I forgot that Ashley's mother was quietly waiting on her turn to complain to Ashley about getting kicked out of her apartment because Jackie's crusty ass stopped sending her monthly checks. "I came all the way here to let you know, not only am I homeless, I have no more savings because your nothing-ass son stole my life savings. I don't know where he's hiding out at. Soon as I lay my eyes on Stud, I'm putting my foot right in his stank ass."

"Momma, I can't believe Stud did you so dirty."

"A girl by the name of Tina informed me that he was gonna try to go upstate and hide out with you, so I came all the way here so I can get my money back, and to lay up off of you for once."

"Momma, shit is really crazy over here. Bill informed me that I was on borrowed time staying in his house."

"From what I just heard, Bill has no authority to kick you out. Ashley, fuck the dumb shit, what's been going on? Ashley, let me find out that your musty ass has been fucking on another woman's husband. One day, Ashley, somebody's gonna make you meet your maker. Damn, bitch, learn how to keep your legs closed."

"Momma, shit is complicated. Don't worry, me and Kim have really gotten close."

"Kim, I don't know what type of weird shit you got going on around here, but I need to rest. Me and your father was driving all night. And to think that we came all this way and you're running around here looking like trash."

While I was explaining to my parents that I don't currently live in the mansion anymore, Bill, Jackie, and Eric had the nerve to interrupt our private conversation by informing my parents that I got kicked out because I was the town slut.

"Jackie, fuck you."

"No, fuck you, Kim. I hope and pray that your parents came all this way to come get your nothing ass. You've been a dirty-ass cunt since the day my boy came to my home and had the nerve to tell me that he married such trash. My son wants to front here and act like he married in the family way. Bitches, I hate to fuck up y'all's little party, but this empire belongs to Eric and myself. Let me inform all of you unfortunate creatures that I don't fraternize with the poor. Let me write y'all down-on-your-luck-ass motherfuckers a check, because I'm tired of looking at y'all's musty asses."

"Jackie, just cut me and my husband a check and we'll be getting up out of your dusty-ass house."

"Jackie, just write me a check too for my pain and suffering. I know you know that my own daughter got herself pregnant by both of my husbands. I feel so sorry for your family, Jackie. Ashley doesn't mind humping her way through your family. Jackie, you better watch Ashley, she might start fucking on your husband."

"I'm not worried about your daughter fucking my husband. Your daughter is a full-fledged crackhead. My husband would never."

"Ashley, when did you start that nasty crackhead habit?"

"She must've started sniffing coke when her and Kim walked out on their own babies."

"Bitch, stop lying to my mother and father."

"Kim, you know I have no reason to be lying. Why would I lie to the poor? Kim, your poor-ass family is all up in my family home trying to collect a check from me. Your trifling daughter left my precious grandson because she found out that my son is just as broke as she is, and Kim couldn't handle that, so your goofy-ass daughter went on a mission. Kim and Ashley went slutting for months. Y'all goofy-ass grown-adult kids thought their dimes and nickels were slick. They knew that I would always stand up for my family. I even had my lawyers draw up documents that gave me full custody of all my grandkids."

"Jackie, you never informed me that you gained custody rights to Bill Junior."

"Kim, at the time it wasn't none of your damn business."

In the process of Jackie telling our parents how we made a lot of mistakes by dumping our kids off on her, in came Jackie's security team, shoving Stud to the ground and they had Amanda's gut-ass in a headlock. Amanda must have tried to jump slick because they had a tight grip around her neck.

"Why in the hell are you strong-arming my granddaughter? Why in the hell is this young punk sitting under my roof untouched? Amanda, I know you ain't got this young punk all up in my home stealing?"

"Mrs. King, I found your granddaughter and this young punk all up in your and Eric's room with a bag full of jewelry, clothes, and they attempted to mess with the safe, your alarm went off."

Before anyone got the message, Bill leaped up and slapped the nine-liter juice out of Amanda. Before he could put hands and feet on Stud, the police came marching in. Jackie made sure to inform the police that Stud just got done robbing his own grandmother.

"Damn, Bill, look what you brought into the world! That little bitch was willing to rob from her own family so she could take care of that trash."

"Momma, the police saved Amanda's life. I even started to chicken-choke the shit out of Stud. That motherfucker needs a slow ass-whooping. That hood punk thinks that he can come all up in my family's home and fuck on my wife and my daughter."

"Bill, stop harping about my love life. Nobody said anything to you when you started fucking on Megan, Ashley, and God knows who else. Just mind your motherfucking business, Bill. Kim, I don't mean no harm or disrespect, but I'm so tired of all this back and forth. Jackie, just cut us a check and we will respectfully get the fuck out of this dysfunctional hellhole that you call a home."

"Kim and Ashley, explain to your misguided family members that you're financially fucked up. Please don't come to my home trying to make me and my husband feel bad because y'all are down bad."

I had to remove myself from Kim and Ashley's situation because I heard glass breaking upstairs. I already knew who that was.

Momma. While trying to calm my crazy mother down because she was still in her feelings over Ashley stealing her cocaine. Whenever Momma was on her high, she always cussed my ass out from here to across the street. When I mentioned to Momma that she was gonna detox today, she lost her whole motherfucking mind. Momma even threatened to slice me up. Before she could make her threats a reality, Jackie's bodyguard came in and tackled Momma down like she was a football player. As ordered, I informed Jackie's bodyguards that I didn't want Momma to come out of her suite until she detoxed.

I already knew I had another task on the way downstairs. It sounded like I had to calm them batty motherfuckers down that sounded like they were about to get it popping at any minute. I also noticed Momma showed a little emotion for once in her life. Momma had a few tears coming down her face. Momma had been addicted to cocaine for so long. The thought about detoxing scared the shit out of her.

Damn, the Lord was on Kim's side because if I didn't come downstairs when I did, Jackie was gonna send Kim to meet her maker. Jackie had picked up a wine bottle and was inches away from clocking Kim in her head.

"Jackie, what's gotten into you? Jackie, why would you risk going to prison, and then poor little Bill Junior would become an orphan?"

"Kim, you better get your French 'wannabe' ass the fuck out of my home. I was really trying to be nice by informing these poor, uneducated creatures that they weren't welcomed at my home, and this bitch lost her mind and told me that her and her parents weren't going anywhere."

"Jackie and Eric, please let Kim and Ashley's parents stay? There's plenty of room at the cottage. I know you don't wanna hear this, Jackie, but we're all family. I'm letting you know right now, Jackie, if you kick Kim's parents out, I promise you that I'm moving out."

"Megan, please calm down, you're talking crazy."

"I'm not talking crazy for once, I'm standing up for everybody. If I got to stay in this loveless home, we're gonna need family around. Jackie, my mother is honestly, in my mind, the worst person on earth, but I'm more than happy that you've let my crazy mother stay on the property."

"Megan, stop your worrying, you know me and Eric will do anything for you."

"Mom, what the hell are you talking about? There's no room in my small cottage for Kim and Ashley's extended fucked-up family."

"Listen, Bill, you already know whatever Megan wants, she gets, and don't expect me to go back and forth with you."

"Jackie and Eric, it's time for bed. I got some strawberries and whipped cream upstairs for y'all. Kim, Ashley, give me twenty minutes and I'll meet y'all at our pond, let me put these senior citizens to bed."

"Megan, you see Bill over there, madder than a bitch. He's just mad because I won't let him taste my pussy. Megan, I don't think anybody wants Bill's weak-ass dick anymore. Let's make moves, I have to pretend like I'm enjoying Jackie and Eric's crazy sex life."

"Okay, we'll see you in a minute at the pond. I love you girls with my whole life."

EPILOGUE

SIXTEENTEEN YEARS LATER:

ONE HORRIBLE BAD DREAM:

"Bitch, get your ass out of my closet!"

"Mya, stop being stingy, you know you got the best clothes. Damn, Bill Junior, every time you came out of the closet, your ass been trying to get all up in everything that I own."

"Mya, let me please rock your Prada shirt to school tomorrow?"

"I guess. You better be glad I fucks with you."

"So I heard through the grapevine, Mya, that Grandpa Eric is on his last leg?"

"I know. Momma Jackie, Megan, Kim, and Ashley have been pacing back and forth by his room checking on him constantly. Our family doctor informed Momma Jackie that Papa won't make it through the night. Kim informed me that as soon as Grandpa dies, you will inherit everything, and my father won't get nothing but a few million dollars and our family cottage. I'm so tired of your father blaming me for being alive and Papa leaving me everything in his will. Bitch, I don't have time to focus on my hating-ass brother, I have a date with Michael's fine ass, and before I start my grieving process, I would like to get me some dick."

"Mya, ask Michael if he has any gay homeboys?"

"Bitch, get your own fuckboys. I have a funeral soon coming up, I don't have time to be nobody's matchmaker. Where are your brothers? They are the ones that has all the homeboys."

"Bitch, just forget it, I'll find my own fuckboys."

That's when we heard screaming from every angle in the house. Papa Eric has finally met his maker. Megan tried consoling me, but we were never that close, and I made sure to remove her hand from my shoulder. I still didn't understand how Momma Jackie had Papa's hoe in her home as long as she did. Damn, I can't wait until Papa's long-ass funeral was over. I was just over people. How many times did I have to hear that they were sorry for my loss? Momma Jackie must have caught me being slick with one of Papa's longtime friends and she came over to tell me to cut it out before she dotted my eye. Momma Jackie was the only one in the world that had enough nerve to put me in my place.

Just like clockwork, my family always had to show their ass. Kim and Bill Junior got into it because she noticed that he had on her brand-new Gucci dress. Ashley was about to chicken-choke Corey because ten minutes before Papa's funeral, Corey got caught having a threesome with Jackie's maids. I was just over Megan's phony ass. This bitch got the nerve to be sitting in the front like she was his wife. If it was up to me, she would've had her dusty ass in the back. Right after the funeral, our family lawyer came to the house to inform me that I inherited everything. Momma Jackie had to get her bodyguard because Bill started throwing shit and started calling me all kind of bastards, and I didn't give three fucks because Bill had been calling me a bastard all my life. Bill had already known that Papa was leaving me all his money, so I didn't get why he was tripping. While Momma Jackie's bodyguard had Bill in a chokehold, I made sure to be funny and remind him that he was the help now.

I sure didn't want anybody going to sleep until we all had a family meeting. Kim's stank ass always had to be funny. "What the fuck do we have to sit around each other for? I'm about to put my foot in Bill Junior's ass for stretching out my new Gucci dress."

"I'm just letting Megan, Kim, Ashley, and Bill know that their services on my property were over. I made sure to inform their down-on-their-luck asses that I don't know where they were going, but they had to get the fuck off my land. Momma Jackie tried to get me to let Megan stay. Momma, it's been time for Megan's hoe ass to be getting the fuck out of my home. Megan, I hope you and your posse saved up y'all's coins because all of you will need every dime."

That's when Megan leaped across the table and started choking the shit out of my neck. Corey and Bill Junior tried to help me, but Megan's grip was too tight. That's when Kim and Ashley started jumping on their boys and reminding them that they came out of their womb and that they weren't going anywhere. We all literally fought for two hours. Blood was everywhere. I had about three speed knots, my nose was bleeding. I also had Megan's handprint around my neck. Bill Junior and Corey got cracked upside the head with a few pots and pans, and I guess you know Kim ripped her Gucci dress off of Bill Junior. Ashley made sure to kick Corey in his private area.

Just like always, Momma Jackie saved their motherfucking lives. "If y'all don't get your bat-shit crazy, fucked-up-in-the-head, disrespectful, punk asses upstairs right now... Now that y'all showed your entire ass today, Papa Eric would be rolling around in his grave if he knew that his daughter and grandkids would actually try and put their own parents out on the side of the road."

"Momma Jackie, fuck that bitch, I always had a problem with Megan since birth."

Bill Junior and Corey even stood up to Momma Jackie. "Momma, we never meant to be disrespectful, but our mothers never gave a fuck about us."

"I still want you kids hating your parents with so much anger. Your parents tried to become productive humans but their parents fucked them up."

While trying to convince the kids to let their parents remain on the property, Kim's stank ass gonna scream out, "Let's go for a second round! I sure don't mind dotting my boy right in the eye."

"Enough is enough, I'm still in charge of this crazy family. Nobody will be getting kicked out. Your mothers reminded me a long time ago about family. We're not perfect but we're still family."

www.ingramcontent.com/pod-product-compliance
Lightning Source LLC
Chambersburg PA
CBHW040836010826
48978CB00012BB/778